PJ MASKS SAVE THE SKY

Based on the episodes "Protector of the Sky" and "Villain of the Sky"

Simon Spotlight
New York London Toronto Sydney New Delhi

S0-AJI-317

SIMON SPOTLIGHT
An imprint of Simon & Schuster Children's Publishing Division
1230 Avenue of the Americas, New York, New York 10020
This Simon Spotlight edition October 2020
This book is based on the TV series PJ MASKS © Frog Box / Entertainment One UK Limited / Walt Disney EMEA Productions Limited 2014;
Les Pyjamasques by Romuald © (2007) Gallimard Jeunesse. All Rights Reserved. This book/publication © Entertainment One UK Limited 2020.
Adapted by Patty Michaels from the series PJ Masks
All rights reserved, including the right of reproduction in whole or in part in any form.
SIMON SPOTLIGHT and colophon are registered trademarks of Simon & Schuster, Inc.
For information about special discounts for bulk purchases, please contact Simon & Schuster Special Sales at 1-866-506-1949 or business@simonandschuster.com.
Manufactured in China 0720 SDI

Amaya, Connor, and Greg are walking home when Greg notices something wrong. "Why is there a hole where a street lamp used to be?" he asks.

Other metal parts from the city are missing too.

"I sense trouble," Amaya says. "PJ Masks, we're on our way!
Into the night to save the day!"

Connor becomes Catboy!

Greg becomes Gekko!

Amaya becomes Owlette!

They are the PJ Masks!

At HQ the PJ Masks see flying robots on the Picture Player. That means one thing: Romeo! Owlette notices that PJ Robot looks just like the flying robots. Maybe he could spy on Romeo and figure out what he is up to.

PJ Robot sneaks into Romeo's new factory. Romeo must be using the city's metal parts for the factory, but what does the factory do?

Just then Romeo decides to inspect all his robots, and he finds PJ Robot!

"Seize him!" Romeo yells. PJ Robot is trapped!

The PJ Masks enter the factory to rescue PJ Robot.

"Super Cat Speed!" Catboy says as he races past a flying robot.

"Super Gekko Shield!" Gekko says, defending himself from robot lasers.

The PJ Masks aren't able to figure out Romeo's plan yet, but at least they are able to save their friend and go back to HQ.

Romeo's factory begins to rumble and takes off into the sky. It turns out that his newest invention is a Flying Factory! The Flying Factory begins to release stinky clouds of gunk.

"To the Owl Glider!" Owlette says. But she wants PJ Robot to stay at HQ. She doesn't want to risk him being captured again.

Romeo spots the Owl Glider flying toward him. "Release more gunk!" he tells his robots in the control room. The robots type away, and the Flying Factory releases more clouds into the sky.

The PJ Masks try to dodge the clouds, but the clouds are so sticky! Soon the Owl Glider is covered with gunk, and it has trouble flying.

Owlette jumps out of the Owl Glider and wants to head to the Flying Factory by herself.

Owlette's wings become covered in yucky gunk too. She tries to use her Super Owl Feathers against Romeo, but nothing happens.

"Poor Owlette," Romeo laughs. "No magical feathers, and she can't really fly either!"

Romeo's robot captures Owlette before tossing her back into the air. "Whoa!" she cries. Then she notices the sky blowing some of the gunk off her wings. The clean air in the sky is helping to remove the gunk!

Owlette manages to land safely on the ground next to Catboy and Gekko. They have been forced to land the Owl Glider, and now everyone is stranded on the ground.

Owlette looks up at a clearing in the sky. If she can get to the clean air, it might remove the rest of the gunk from her wings. Then she can regain her powers and fly again!

Catboy and Gekko wonder if there is a different and better way to take on the Flying Factory. But Owlette is determined to get her wings back.

The PJ Masks try to use the Gekko-Mobile to launch Owlette into the air. But she just gets covered in gunk again.

"Everything is gunked!" Owlette cries. "The sky, my cape, and my powers!"

Gekko tries to use his Super Gekko Muscles to remove the gunk off her wings, but it doesn't work.

Then Catboy realizes something. The Flying Factory has a vacuum to suck up all the metal parts from the city. "Maybe it could suck up not just metal . . . but the gunk clouds, too!" he says.

"But that means getting into the factory's control room," Gekko says. "How can we do that if Owlette can't fly?"

"No more worrying about my wings," Owlette tells Catboy and Gekko. "I'll fix this with your help. It's time to be a hero!"
Catboy uses his Super Cat Stripes to make a catapult. It launches them to the Flying Factory.

Romeo has no idea the PJ Masks are on their way. "At last, we're ready!" he announces. "Double turbo super gunk mode! Power up in 3, 2 . . ."

The Flying Factory's vacuum sucks up all the gunk clouds from the sky, and the sky begins to clear.

"It's working!" Gekko says. The PJ Masks have defeated Romeo's Flying Factory!

With the sky cleared up, Owlette can use her powers again too.
"Go, Owlette! Protector of the sky!" Catboy cheers.
"Protector of the sky?" Owlette says, smiling. "Maybe. But I couldn't have done it without my friends!"

PJ Masks all shout hooray, 'cause in the night,
they saved the sky . . . *and* the day!